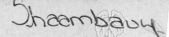

D0504511

A Peter Rabbit Tale

Miss Moppet

Based on the original story by
Beatrix Potter
with all new illustrations

Cover illustration by
Anita Nelson
Book illustrations by
Pat Schoonover

Publications International, Ltd.

This is the story of Miss Moppet. Do you know why her eyes look so big? She thinks she has heard a mouse!

This is the mouse peeping out from behind the cupboard and making fun of Miss Moppet. He is not afraid of a kitten.

This is Miss Moppet jumping just a little too late. She misses the mouse and hits her own head. She thinks it is a very hard cupboard!

Meanwhile, the mouse watches Miss Moppet from the top of the cupboard.

Miss Moppet ties her head up in a handkerchief and sits before the fire. The mouse thinks Miss Moppet is hurt. He comes sliding down the draperies to get a closer look. Miss Moppet looks worse and worse. The mouse comes a little nearer.

Miss Moppet holds her poor head in her paws. Then she peeks at the mouse through a hole in the handkerchief. The mouse comes very close.

And then—all of a sudden—
Miss Moppet pounces on the
mouse! She catches him by his
little tail!

Because the mouse has teased
Miss Moppet, Miss Moppet
thinks she will tease the mouse.
That is not a nice thing to do.

Miss Moppet ties him up in
the handkerchief and tosses it
about like a ball.

But she has forgotten about that hole in the handkerchief. When she unties the handkerchief— there is no mouse!

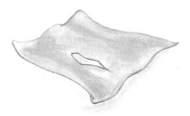

He has wriggled out and run away. Now he is dancing a jig on the top of the cupboard!

Miss Moppet has given up for today. For now, she'll rest. Perhaps she will dream of having just a little bit better luck. Tomorrow is a new day!